An I Can Read
Picture Book™

DANNY
and the
DINOSAUR

Story and Pictures
by Syd Hoff

BARNES & NOBLE
NEW YORK

Danny and the Dinosaur
Copyright © 1958 by Syd Hoff
Copyright renewed 1986 by Syd Hoff

This 2005 edition licensed for publication by Barnes & Noble Publishing, Inc., by arrangement with
HarperCollins Publishers.

HarperCollins Publishers® is a registered trademark.

Barnes & Noble Publishing, Inc.
122 Fifth Avenue
New York, NY 10011

ISBN 0-7607-6502-2
Manufactured in China
07 08 09 MCH 10 9 8 7 6 5

DANNY and the DINOSAUR

One day Danny went to the museum.

He wanted to see what was inside.

He saw Indians.

He saw bears.

He saw Eskimos.

He saw guns.

He saw swords.

And he saw . . .

DINOSAURS!

Danny loved dinosaurs.

He wished he had one.

"I'm sorry they are not real," said Danny.
"It would be nice to play with a dinosaur."
"And I think it would be nice to play with
you," said a voice.

"Can you?" said Danny.

"Yes," said the dinosaur.

"Oh, good," said Danny. "What can we do?"

"I can take you for a ride," said the dinosaur.
He put his head down so Danny could get on him.

"Let's go!" said Danny.

A policeman stared at them.

He had never seen a dinosaur stop for a red light.

The dinosaur was so tall Danny had to hold up
the ropes for him.

"Look out!" said Danny.

"Bow wow!" said a dog.

"He thinks you are a car," said Danny.

"Go away, dog. We are not a car."

"I can make a noise like a car," said the dinosaur.

"Honk! Honk! Honk!"

"What big rocks," said the dinosaur.

"They are not rocks," said Danny. "They are buildings."

"I love to climb," said the dinosaur.
"Down, boy!" said Danny.

The dinosaur had to be very careful not to knock over houses or stores with his long tail.

Some people were waiting for a bus.
They rode on the dinosaur's tail instead.

"All who want to cross the street may walk on my back," said the dinosaur.

"It's very nice of you to help me with my bundles," said a lady.

Danny and the dinosaur went all over town
and had lots of fun.

"It's good to take an hour or two off after
a hundred million years," said the dinosaur.

They even looked at the ball game.

"Hit the ball," said Danny.

"Hit a home run," said the dinosaur.

"I wish we had a boat," said Danny.

"Who needs a boat? I can swim," said the dinosaur.

"Toot, toot!" went the boats.

"Toot, toot!" went Danny and the dinosaur.

"Oh, what lovely green grass!" said the dinosaur.
"I haven't eaten any of that
for a very long time."
"Wait," said Danny.
"See what it says."

PLEASE
KEEP
OFF

They both had ice cream instead.

"Let's go to the zoo and see the animals," said Danny.

Everybody came running to see the dinosaur.

Nobody stayed to see the lions.

Nobody stayed to see the elephants.

Nobody stayed to see the monkeys.

And nobody stayed to see the seals,
giraffes or hippos, either.

"Please go away so the animals will get looked at," said the zoo man.

"Let's find my friends," said Danny.

"Very well," said the dinosaur.

"There they are," said Danny.

"Why, it's Danny riding on a dinosaur," said a child.

"Maybe he'll give us a ride."

"May we have a ride?" asked the children.

"I'd be delighted," said the dinosaur.

"Hold on tight," said Danny.

Around and around the block ran the dinosaur, faster and faster and faster.

"This is better than a merry-go-round," the children said.

The dinosaur was out of breath.

"Teach him tricks," said the children.

Danny taught the dinosaur how to shake hands.

"Can you roll over on your back?" asked the children.

"That's easy," said the dinosaur.

"He's smart," said Danny, patting the dinosaur.

"Let's play hide and seek," said the children.

"How do you play it?" said the dinosaur.

"We hide and you try to find us," said Danny.

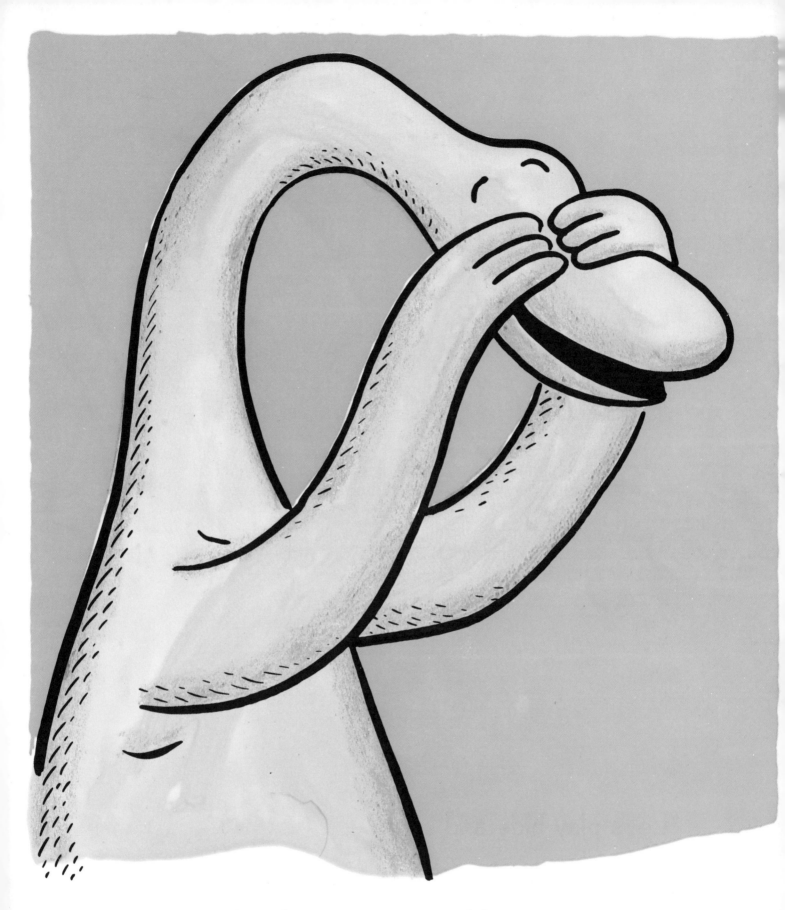

The dinosaur covered his eyes.

All the children ran to hide.

The dinosaur looked and looked but he couldn't find the children.

"I give up," he said.

Now it was the dinosaur's turn to hide.
The children covered their eyes.

The dinosaur hid behind a house.
The children found him.

He hid behind a sign.
The children found him.

He hid behind a big gas tank.

The children found him.

They found him again and again and again.

"I guess there's no place for me to hide," said
the dinosaur.
"Let's make believe we can't find him," Danny said.

"Where can he be?

Where, oh, where is that dinosaur?

Where did he go?

We give up," said the children.

"Here I am," said the dinosaur.

"The dinosaur wins," said the children.
"We couldn't find him. He fooled us."

"Hurrah for the dinosaur!" the children cried.
"Hurray! Hurray!"

It got late and the other children left.
Danny and the dinosaur were alone.

"Well, goodbye, Danny," said the dinosaur.

"Can't you come and stay with me?" said Danny. "We could have fun."

"No," said the dinosaur. "I've had a good time— the best I've had in a hundred million years. But now I must get back to the museum. They need me there."

"Oh," said Danny. "Well, goodbye."

Danny watched until the long tail was out of sight.

Then he went home alone.

"Oh, well," thought Danny, "we don't have room for a pet that size, anyway. But we did have a wonderful day."